To my daddy

love from

....

First published in paperback in Great Britain by HarperCollins Children's Books in 2006
This edition published in 2013

1 3 5 7 9 10 8 6 4 2

ISBN: 978-0-00-750866-2

HarperCollins Children's Books is a division of HarperCollins Publishers Ltd.
Text and illustrations copyright © HarperCollins Publishers Ltd 2006

Visit our website at: www.harpercollins.co.uk

Printed and bound in China

Why I Love My Daddy

Illustrated by Daniel Howarth

HarperCollins *Children's Books*

I love my daddy because...

he is big and strong.

I love my daddy because...

he is clever.

I love my daddy because...
he keeps me safe and cosy.

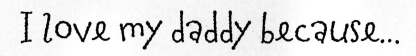

I love my daddy because...

he plays with me.

I love my daddy because...

he carries me.

I love my daddy because...

he is handsome.

I love my daddy because...

he is funny.

I love my daddy because...
he hugs me good night.

I love my daddy because...
he fixes things.

I love my daddy because...
he tickles me.

I love my daddy because...

he is kind.

I love my daddy because...

he has the best ideas.

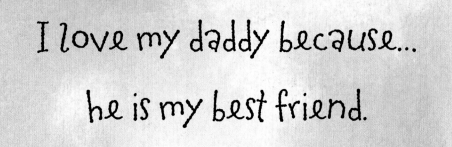

I love my daddy because...
he is my best friend.

Everyone loves
their daddy –

especially...

ME!